Y0-DWN-295

Lee Aucoin, *Creative Director*
Jamey Acosta, *Senior Editor*
Heidi Fiedler, *Editor*
Produced and designed by
Denise Ryan & Associates
Illustration © Sarah S. Brannen
Rachelle Cracchiolo, *Publisher*

Teacher Created Materials
5301 Oceanus Drive
Huntington Beach, CA 92649-1030
http://www.tcmpub.com
Paperback: ISBN: 978-1-4333-5568-4
Library Binding: ISBN: 978-1-4807-1713-8
© 2014 Teacher Created Materials

Sarah's Journal

Written by Helen Bethune
Illustrated by Sarah S. Brannen

Saturday, April 15, 1634

Dear Diary,

We're sailing to the New World. We are leaving England forever and sailing to ~~Massachoo~~ ~~Masachusets~~ Massachusetts to make a new life for ourselves. It will take nearly two months to cross the Atlantic if the weather is fair. That's eight weeks! We're going to stay with Mother's cousins in Salem until we can buy some land for ourselves.

ELIZABETH

The motion of the waves is making me feel ill. Mother is too busy with the younger children to pay heed to me. She wants me to help her. Mary should do that but she seems to be unwell. I think she's making it up to avoid her duties. Father is talking to the ship's master, Mr. Andrewes.

Sarah

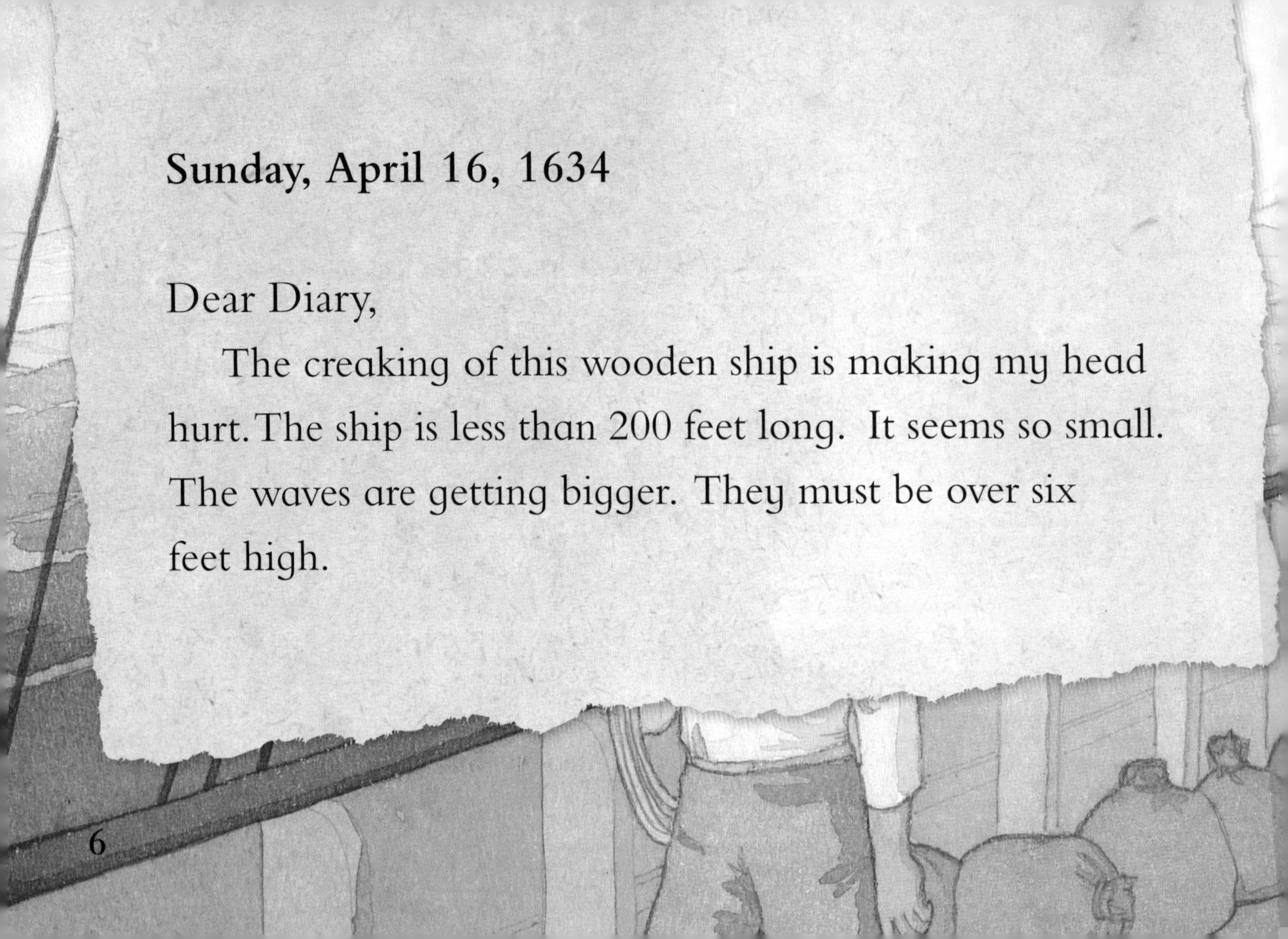

Sunday, April 16, 1634

Dear Diary,

The creaking of this wooden ship is making my head hurt. The ship is less than 200 feet long. It seems so small. The waves are getting bigger. They must be over six feet high.

This cabin is so cramped. There is hardly enough room for us and our belongings. We try to sleep in boxes that hold us like cradles. At least we don't fall out. They are about five feet long, long enough for me but not for Father. I'm frightened, I want to go home, and now I feel most unwell.

Sarah

Thursday, June 1, 1634

Dear Diary,

We finally reached land. I never thought we would. I thought I was going to die. I thought we were all going to die. Mother, the little ones, and I were sick all the way. And so was Mary. Father was not sick. I think his joy in going to the New World overcomes all else.

I am so glad to be off the ship, after nearly nine weeks at sea. Our cousins met our ship. We made our way by horse and wagon to Salem, where they live. The journey was almost 15 miles.

Sarah

I was quite shocked by the house. It has dirt floors and bark walls. Life is so different here. Father says we are lucky to be able to make a new life for ourselves. We are blessed.

Sarah

Thursday, August 3, 1634

Dear Diary,

Cousin Daniel says I must keep writing my thoughts in my journal. Maybe then I won't say what I'm thinking. It makes Mother and Father so cross with me, as I'm afraid I do not like it here. I miss my friends. The town is not a town at all. It is like a camp.

The only real building is the meeting house. We spend all of Sunday and several hours each Wednesday there, listening to the pastor talk for hours. Sometimes I fall asleep, but Mother shakes me awake. Afterwards, we play on the village green. Here is a drawing of the village green and the meeting house.

Sarah

Thursday, August 17, 1634

Dear Diary,

I am overjoyed! Father has at last bought some land. It already has a house on it, and I shall only have to share my bed with Emily. Our new home is six miles from Salem, but Father has promised we shall each have a pony. We will be able to ride in to see our cousins. And, of course to go to the meeting house. We are all so eager to move to our own home. I expect our cousins shall be glad, too.

Sarah

Monday, August 28, 1634

Dear Diary,

We have planted the first of our corn. In about six weeks the plants shall be grown. The Indians have been very helpful in showing us ways to work the soil and telling us what we should plant. Without their help, we may have starved. We now have eight hens and a cow. I must milk the cow each morning.

Sarah

Monday, September 4, 1634

Dear Diary,

I have started attending school. It is held in a bare room with only chalk, pencils, and very little paper. There aren't any chalkboards. To write, Mr. Crawford uses a stick of charcoal on a piece of birch bark from the tree. He makes gallons of ink for our goose quills.

Sarah

Maſſachuſetts
Bay
Bostn

November 21, 1634

Dear Diary,

At last I can say I am enjoying life in the New World. I love Darcy, my pony. The school is half a mile away. Claire and Susan are the best friends a girl could ever have. Our teacher is teaching us about our great colony, Massachusetts. Our crops have grown, and I don't think it possible that our hens could lay any more eggs.

I have much to be thankful for.

Sarah